Congratulations on choosing the best in educational materials for your child. By selecting top-quality McGraw-Hill products, you can be assured that the concepts used in our books will reinforce and enhance the skills that are being taught in classrooms nationwide.

And what better way to get young readers excited than with Mercer Mayer's Little Critter, a character loved by children everywhere? Our First Readers offer simple and engaging stories about Little Critter that children can read on their own. Each level incorporates reading skills, colorful illustrations, and challenging activities.

Level 1 – The stories are simple and use repetitive language. Illustrations are highly supportive.
Level 2 - The stories begin to grow in complexity. Language is still repetitive, but it is mixed with more challenging vocabulary.
Level 3 - The stories are more complex. Sentences are longer and more varied.

To help your child make the most of this book, look at the first few pictures in the story and discuss what is happening. Ask your child to predict where the story is going. Then, once your child has read the story, have him or her review the word list and do the activities. This will reinforce vocabulary words from the story and build reading comprehension.

You are your child's first and most influential teacher. No one knows your child the way you do. Tailor your time together to reinforce a newly acquired skill or to overcome a temporary stumbling block. Praise your child's progress and ideas, take delight in his or her imagination, and most of all, enjoy your time together!

Library of Congress Cataloging-in-Publication Data

Mayer, Mercer, 1943-
   Our friend Sam / by Mercer Mayer.
       p. cm. – (First readers, skills and practice)
   Summary: Little Critter and Gabby find a caterpillar in the yard, and they take care of it until it turns
into a beautiful butterfly and flies away. Includes activities.
   PB ISBN 1-57768-815-5
   HC ISBN 1-57768-458-3
      [1. Caterpillars—Fiction. 2. Butterflies—Fiction.] I. Title. II. Series.

PZ7.M462 Ou 2001
[E]—dc21   2001031211

Mc Graw Hill Children's Publishing

Text Copyright © 2002 McGraw-Hill Children's Publishing.
Art Copyright © 2002 Mercer Mayer.

Send all inquiries to:
McGraw-Hill Children's Publishing
8787 Orion Place
Columbus, OH 43240-4027

Printed in the United States of America.
PB 1-57768-815-5
HC 1-57768-458-3

1 2 3 4 5 6 7 8 9 10 PHXBK 06 05 04 03 02

 A Big Tuna Trading Company, LLC/J. R. Sansevere Book

The McGraw-Hill Companies

FIRST READERS

Level **3**   Grades **1–2**

OUR FRIEND SAM

by Mercer Mayer

Mc Graw Hill **Children's Publishing**

Columbus, Ohio

One day, Gabby and I were playing tag in my yard. I looked down and saw something in the grass. It was a little black caterpillar.

The caterpillar crawled on my finger.
Then he crawled on my hand.
I called him Sam and brought
him inside.

"Mom, Dad, look! I have a
new pet," I said.

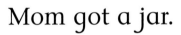

Mom got a jar.

Dad put holes in the lid for air.

Gabby and I went outside to pick
leaves for Sam to eat.

9

I kept Sam in my room. Every afternoon,
Gabby and I took Sam outside.
He zigzagged through the grass.
Sometimes he crawled up and down
Gabby's back.

One afternoon, Gabby and I
went to my room to get Sam.
He had made a cocoon around himself.
He was hanging from the lid of the jar.
"Soon Sam will be a butterfly,"
said Gabby.

In a few days, Sam came out
of his cocoon. He was
a beautiful orange butterfly!
Gabby and I took him outside.
We opened the jar. Sam flew out
and landed on my hand.

15

"I'm going to miss Sam,"
I said to Gabby.
Gabby said, "Sam is going to
find his butterfly friends."
I said, "I hope Sam finds
a nice friend like you, Gabby."

Word List

Read each word in the lists below. Then, find each word in the story. Now, make up a new sentence using the word. Say your sentence out loud.

Words I Know
yard
grass
caterpillar
hand
jar
leaves
butterfly

Challenge Words
finger
brought
crawled
cocoon
beautiful

Comprehension Quiz

Answer these questions without looking back at the story.

What color was the caterpillar?

What did Little Critter name the caterpillar?

What did the caterpillar eat?

What did the caterpillar make around himself?

What did the caterpillar turn into?

What color was the butterfly?

Short I

On a separate sheet of paper, change or add a letter (or letters) to the beginning of each word below to make new words. Keep the short i sound. The first one has been done for you.

in ⟶ bin, fin, gin, pin, sin, tin, win, chin, thin, spin

it ⟶ ?

him ⟶ ?

lid ⟶ ?

pick ⟶ ?

Pronouns

Pronouns are words that take the place of nouns. They include I, he, she, it, they, you, we, me, him, her, them, and us.

Point to the picture that matches the pronoun.

she

it

he

they

Caterpillar Questions

Read the questions below. Write your answers on a separate sheet of paper. If you need help, use the page numbers to find the answers in the story.

1. How did the caterpillar move through the grass? (page 10)

2. What did Little Critter feed the caterpillar? (page 9)

3. What did the caterpillar become at the end of the story? (page 15)

4. Gabby is Little Critter's ___? (page 17)

5. What did Little Critter find in the grass? (page 4)

6. What did the caterpillar make around himself? (page 13)

Quotation Marks

Quotation marks go before and after a speaker's words. They look like this " ".

Example:

"Sam is our friend," said Little Critter·

How many quotation marks are in the story?

Now, look at the sentences below. Point to the spots where the quotation marks belong.

1. Little Critter asked, What do caterpillars eat?

2. I wonder who Sam will play with now? said Gabby.

3. Sam is pretty, said Little Sister.

4. Dad replied, These holes will help him breathe.

Answer Key

page 19
Comprehension Quiz

What color was the caterpillar? **black**

What did Little Critter name the caterpillar?
Sam

What did the caterpillar eat? _____
leaves

What did the caterpillar make around himself?
a cocoon

What did the caterpillar turn into?
a butterfly

What color was the butterfly?
orange

page 20
Short I
Sample answers given below.

in ⟶ bin, fin, gin, pin, sin, tin, win, chin, thin, spin

it ⟶ sit, kit, lit, hit, pit, bit, fit

him ⟶ rim, Tim dim, Kim

lid ⟶ slid, did, rid, hid

pick ⟶ sick, tick, Rick, kick, lick

page 21
Pronouns

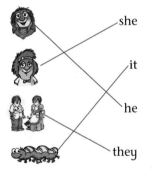

she

it

he

they

page 22
Caterpillar Questions

1. zigzagged
2. leaves
3. butterfly
4. friend
5. caterpillar
6. cocoon

page 23
Quotation Marks

How many quotation marks are in the story? 10

1. Little Critter asked, "What do caterpillars eat?"

2. "I wonder who Sam will play with now?" said Gabby.

3. "Sam is pretty," said Little Sister.

4. Dad replied, "These holes will help him breathe."